SLOOKI
the Sloth

James Thibeau

PAGE PUBLISHING, INC.
Conneaut Lake, PA

First originally published by Page Publishing 2021

ISBN 978-1-6624-4207-0 (pbk)
ISBN 978-1-6624-4209-4 (hc)
ISBN 978-1-6624-4208-7 (digital)

Printed in the United States of America

To my children, Joslyn, Mila, and Alex

Look to your left!
Look to your right!
Slooki the Sloth has a story tonight.

Her story begins in a faraway place
As she searches for talent
and skills to embrace.

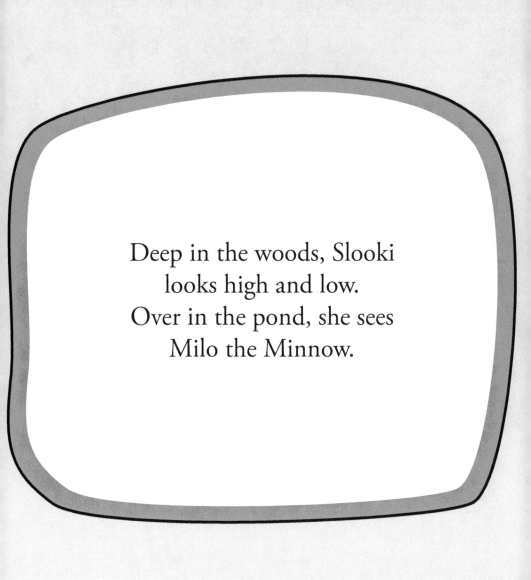

Deep in the woods, Slooki
looks high and low.
Over in the pond, she sees
Milo the Minnow.

Milo can splash. Milo can swim.
Slooki was sad that she was not like him.

Milo assured his friend Slooki so dear,
"Slooki, your talent one day will appear."

7

Slooki gathered herself,
and on she walked,
Who did she see next?
It was Stormy the Stork.

Stormy can stand on her one leg so long.
Stormy can fly with her wings so strong.

Up in the sky, Stormy
soars, and she sings.
Slooki was sad that she
didn't have wings.

Stormy assured her friend Slooki so dear,
"Slooki, your talent one day will appear."

Slooki continued on her
journey so eager.
Who did she see next?
It was Buddy the Beaver!

13

Buddy cuts trees and
builds things so rad.
With one look at his dam,
Slooki began to feel sad.

Buddy assured his friend Slooki so dear,
"Slooki, your talent one day will appear."

15

Slooki strolled on with a feeling so blue,
Hoping the kind words she
heard would come true.

17

Slooki got tired and
stopped under a tree.
She heard a soft voice. It was
Cheeks the Monkey.

19

Hanging so high on a branch in the tree,
Cheeks could swing back
and forth so effortlessly.

Slooki was curious and
wanted a closer look.
So up the tree, she climbed passing
every cranny and nook.

Once at the top, Cheeks turned to say,
"You're just like me, Slooki.
You climb just the same!"

23

Slooki turned to Cheeks
with a smile so bright.
She found her talent, and she
glowed with delight.

Good night!

About the Author

James Thibeau is a father of three, born and raised in Weymouth, Massachusetts. His inspiration to write children's books stems from the vast diversity of his three children, ages range from a toddler, preteen, and full-blown teenage girl. Being a father is the best gift, being able to watch his children overcome challenges and grow is the most rewarding, and he is compelled to share these obstacles through his writing that will help other children find it relatable in their milestones.

CPSIA information can be obtained
at www.ICGtesting.com
Printed in the USA
LVHW070612300921
699020LV00026B/1361

9 781662 442070